Ernie and Hermie visit Earth

Level 3G

Written by Lucy George
Illustrated by Claudia Venturini
Reading Consultant: Betty Franchi

About Phonics

Spoken English uses more than 40 speech sounds. Each sound is called a *phoneme*. Some phonemes relate to a single letter (d-o-g) and others to combinations of letters (sh-ar-p). When a phoneme is written down, it is called a *grapheme*. Teaching these sounds, matching them to their written form, and sounding out words for reading is the basis of phonics.

Early phonics instruction gives children the tools to sound out, blend, and say the words without having to rely on memory or guesswork. This instruction gives children the confidence and ability to read unfamiliar words, helping them progress toward independent reading.

About the Consultant

Betty Franchi is an American educator with
a Bachelor's Degree in Elementary and Middle
Education as well as a Master's Degree in Special
Education. Betty holds a National Boards for
Professional Teaching Standards certification.
Throughout her 24 years as a teacher, she has
studied and developed an expertise in Phonetic
Awareness and has implemented phonetic strategies,
teaching many young children to read, including
students with special needs.

Reading tips

 This book focuses on the *er* sound as in term.

Tricky and/or new words in this book

Any words in bold may have unusual spellings or are new and have not yet been introduced.

> **Tricky and/or new words in this book**
>
> **aimed their zoom first Earth saw iceberg ocean parked what day like care to they the**

Extra ways to have fun with this book

After the readers have finished the story, ask them questions about what they have just read.

What did Hermie do on Earth?
What did Ernie do on Earth?

Explain that the two letters *er* make one sound. Think of other words that make the *er* sound, such as *perm* and *stern*.

This story is out of this world!

A Pronunciation Guide

This grid highlights the sounds used in the story and offers a guide on how to say them.

s	a	t	p	i
as in sat	as in ant	as in tin	as in pig	as in ink
n	c	e	h	r
as in net	as in cat	as in egg	as in hen	as in rat
m	d	g	o	u
as in mug	as in dog	as in get	as in ox	as in up
l	f	b	j	v
as in log	as in fan	as in bag	as in jug	as in van
w	z	y	k	qu
as in wet	as in zip	as in yet	as in kit	as in quick
x	ff	ll	ss	zz
as in box	as in off	as in ball	as in kiss	as in buzz
ck	pp	nn	rr	gg
as in duck	as in puppy	as in bunny	as in arrow	as in egg
dd	bb	tt	sh	ch
as in daddy	as in chubby	as in attic	as in shop	as in chip
th	th	ng	nk	le
as in them	as in the	as in sing	as in sunk	as in bottle
ai	ee	ie	oa	ue
as in rain	as in feet	as in pies	as in oak	as in cue
ar	er			
as in park	as in term			

Be careful not to add an /uh/ sound to /s/, /t/, /p/, /c/, /h/, /r/, /m/, /d/, /g/, /l/, /f/ and /b/. For example, say /fff/ not /fuh/ and /sss/ not /suh/.

Hermie and Ernie **aimed their** ships. **Zoom!**

It was their **first** trip **to Earth**.

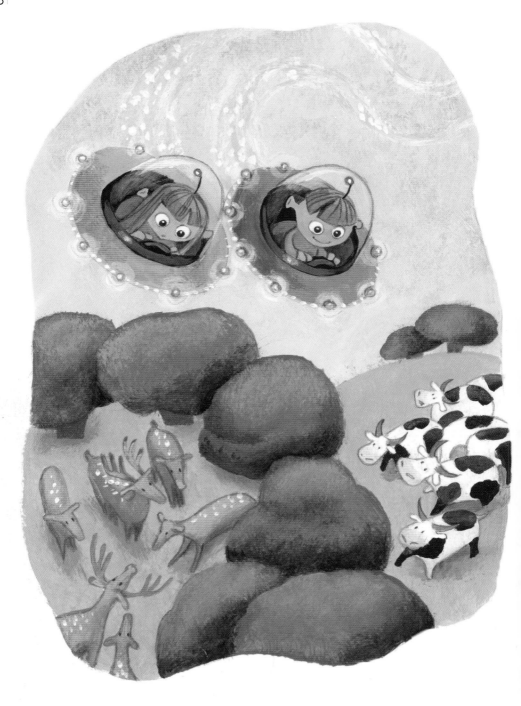

From **the** ships **they saw** herds of elk and oxen.

They passed an **iceberg** and boats on the **ocean**.

Ernie landed his ship
by the curb with a jump.

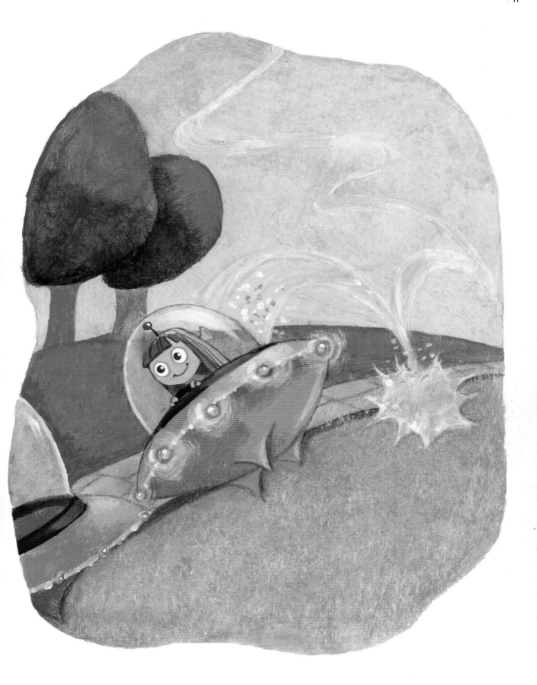

Hermie **parked** her
ship with a jerk.

They went along the curb,
quick and alert.

What should we do
for a **day** on Earth?

14

Hermie wanted a perm.

Her perm was very perky!

"I think you look **like** a nerd!"
Ernie said.

"Buzz off!" she said.
Hermie did not **care**.

Ernie got in line for the opera.

He stood and sang along.

"You cannot sing well,"
Hermie cried. Ernie did not care.

Hermie and Ernie loved their
day on Earth. "It's been a blast!"
they shouted.

Time for takeoff. They raced back.

Ernie sang opera all the way.
Hermie put her fingers in her ears.

OVER 48 TITLES IN SIX LEVELS
Betty Franchi recommends...

Some titles from Level 1

Bad Rat — I love reading phonics
978 1 84898 747 0

The Best Gift — I love reading phonics
978 1 84898 750 0

Clint and Grant Play I-Spy — I love reading phonics
978 1 84898 752 4

Bret and Grandma's Trip! — I love reading phonics
978 1 84898 751 7

Some titles from Level 2

Wish Fish — I love reading phonics
978 1 84898 755 5

Chuck and Duck — I love reading phonics
978 1 84898 756 2

Pink Bunny — I love reading phonics
978 1 84898 760 9

Let's go to the Swings — I love reading phonics
978 1 84898 759 3

Other titles to enjoy from Level 3

GOAT IN A BOAT — I love reading phonics
978 1 84898 766 1

Queen Ella's Feet — I love reading phonics
978 1 84898 764 7

Puff Flies — I love reading phonics
978 1 84898 765 4

An Hachette Company
First Published in the United States by TickTock, an imprint of Octopus Publishing Group.
www.octopusbooksusa.com

Copyright © Octopus Publishing Group Ltd 2013

Distributed in the US by
Hachette Book Group USA
237 Park Avenue, New York NY 10017, USA

Distributed in Canada by
Canadian Manda Group
165 Dufferin Street, Toronto, Ontario, Canada M6K 3H6

ISBN 978 1 84898 769 2

Printed and bound in China
10 9 8 7 6 5 4 3 2 1